# LET'S BE ENEMIES

## by JANICE MAY UDRY

## Pictures by MAURICE SENDAK

HarperTrophy *A Division of* HarperCollins*Publishers*

Let's Be Enemies

Library of Congress Catalog Card Number 61-5777
ISBN 0-06-026130-7
ISBN 0-06-026131-5 (lib. bdg.)
ISBN 0-06-443188-6 (pbk.)

First Harper Trophy edition, 1988.
17 SCP 20 19 18

# LET'S BE
# ENEMIES

James used to be my friend.

But today he is my enemy.

James always wants to be the boss.

James carries the flag.

James takes all the crayons.

He grabs the best digging spoon.

And he throws sand.

So now James is my enemy. Now he hasn't got me for a friend.

When James was my friend
I invited him to my birthday party.

I always shared my pretzels
and my umbrella with him.

I showed him
where the horny toad lives.

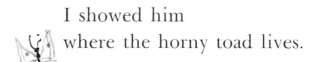

We were such good friends
that we had the chicken pox
together.

But I wouldn't have the chicken pox with James now.

He is my enemy. James *always* wants
to be boss.

I'm going over and poke James.

I think I'll put his crayons
in the soup.

I'm going to tell them not to let
James go to school.
Because he always wants to be boss.

James will think he's the boss
of the whole school.

I'm going right over to James' house
and tell him.

I'm going to tell him
that from now on he is my enemy
and he'll have no one to play with.

"Hullo, James."
"Hullo, John."

"I came to tell you that I'm not
your friend any more."
"Well then, I'm not *your* friend
either."

"We're enemies."
"All right!"

"GOOD-BYE!"
"GOOD-BYE!"

"Hey, James!"

"What?"

"Let's roller-skate."

"O.K. Have a pretzel, John."

"Thank you, James."